Tom and Pippo in the Garden

PIPPO

HELEN OXENBURY

ALADDIN BOOKS
Macmillan Publishing Company • New York

I take Pippo into the garden
a lot. He likes to ride in
my wheelbarrow.

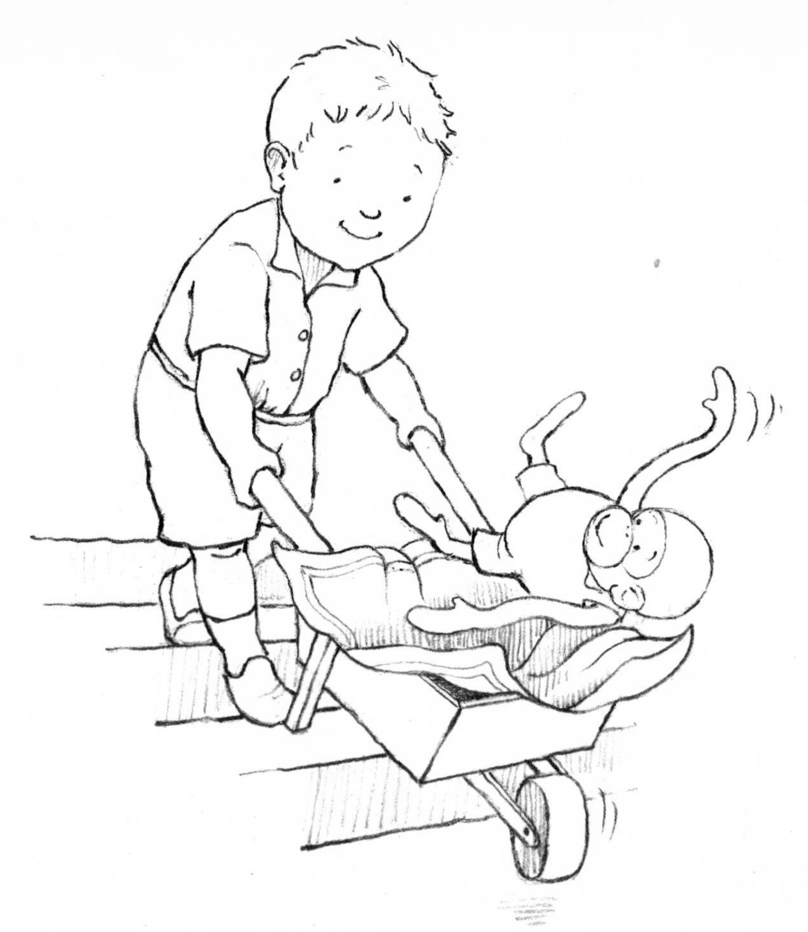

I take him around the paths
and bump him down the steps.
Pippo likes to be bumped.
When we've had enough, I give
him his lunch.

Pippo makes a mess when he eats.
He gets food all over his face.
So I have to wipe him
with a washcloth.

When I hear
Mommy calling,
I make a little bed for Pippo so
he can take a nap while I eat
my lunch.

After lunch,
when we want to play, that cat
is asleep in my wheelbarrow.
We have to shoo him out.

Then I take Pippo around and around the garden until it's time to go in for a snack.